WELCOME TO
PASSPORT TO READING
A beginning reader's ticket to a brand-new world!

Every book in this program is designed to build read-along and read-alone skills, level by level, through engaging and enriching stories. As the reader turns each page, he or she will become more confident with new vocabulary, sight words, and comprehension.

These PASSPORT TO READING levels will help you choose the perfect book for every reader.

READING TOGETHER
Read short words in simple sentence structures together to begin a reader's journey.

READING OUT LOUD
Encourage developing readers to sound out words in more complex stories with simple vocabulary.

READING INDEPENDENTLY
Newly independent readers gain confidence reading more complex sentences with higher word counts.

READY TO READ MORE
Readers prepare for chapter books with ̄ew ̄ illustrations and longer paragraphs.

This book features sight words from t'   e   ̇d Dolch Sight Words List. This encourat ̇es   ̇nize commonly used vocabulary wor   ̇ speed and fluency.

For more information, please visit passpc   .igbooks.com.

Enjoy the journey!

© 2017 MARVEL.
Illustrations by Ron Lim, Andy Smith,
Andy Troy, and Chris Sotomayor

Cover design by Carolyn Bull.

Little, Brown and Company
Hachette Book Group
1290 Avenue of the Americas, New York, NY 10104
Visit us at lb-kids.com
marvelkids.com

First Edition: April 2017

Little, Brown and Company is a division of Hachette Book Group, Inc.
The Little, Brown name and logo are trademarks of Hachette Book Group, Inc.

The publisher is not responsible for websites (or their content) that
are not owned by the publisher.

ISBNs: 978-0-316-27167-7 (pbk.), 978-0-316-55389-6 (ebook),
978-0-316-55388-9 (ebook), 978-0-316-31427-5 (ebook)

Printed in the United States of America

CW

10 9 8 7 6 5 4 3 2 1

Passport to Reading titles are leveled by independent reviewers applying the standards
developed by Irene Fountas and Gay Su Pinnell in *Matching Books to Readers:
Using Leveled Books in Guided Reading*, Heinemann, 1999.

MEET THE TEAM!

Adapted by R. R. Busse
Illustrations by Ron Lim, Andy Smith,
Andy Troy, and Chris Sotomayor
Based on the Major Motion Picture
Written and Directed by James Gunn
Produced by Kevin Feige, p.g.a.

LITTLE, BROWN AND COMPANY
New York   Boston

Attention, GUARDIANS OF THE GALAXY fans! Look for these words when you read this book. Can you spot them all?

mask

monster

asteroid

dancer

These are the Guardians of the Galaxy!

They are heroes in space.

They save beings on far-away planets.

Peter Quill is called Star-Lord.

He is the leader of the Guardians.
He has a very cool mask that
protects him in fights.
He was born on Earth.

Gamora is a great fighter.

She is very serious and very dangerous.

She never breaks a promise.

Drax is a great fighter, too.

He is very strong and likes battles.

He laughs when he fights.

Rocket and Groot are best friends.

Rocket is smart with tools and machines.

Once, Groot was big and brave.

Now he is small and brave.

All he says is "I am Groot."

Ayesha is the leader of the Sovereign. She hires the Guardians to protect batteries that help her planet.

This giant monster wants
to eat the batteries.
The Guardians have to stop it!

The team has to work together.

Even little Groot helps!

The monster is very big and very tough.

Together, the Guardians beat the monster!

Nebula is Gamora's adopted sister.
They do not get along.

Nebula is the prisoner of the Sovereign.
They let her leave with the Guardians
after they beat the monster.

Oh no!

Rocket says he took one of the batteries from Ayesha!

Peter is angry with Rocket...

...but not as angry as Ayesha is!
She sends her ships after the Guardians.
The Guardians have to fly away
in their ship, the Milano.
Luckily, the Milano is very fast.

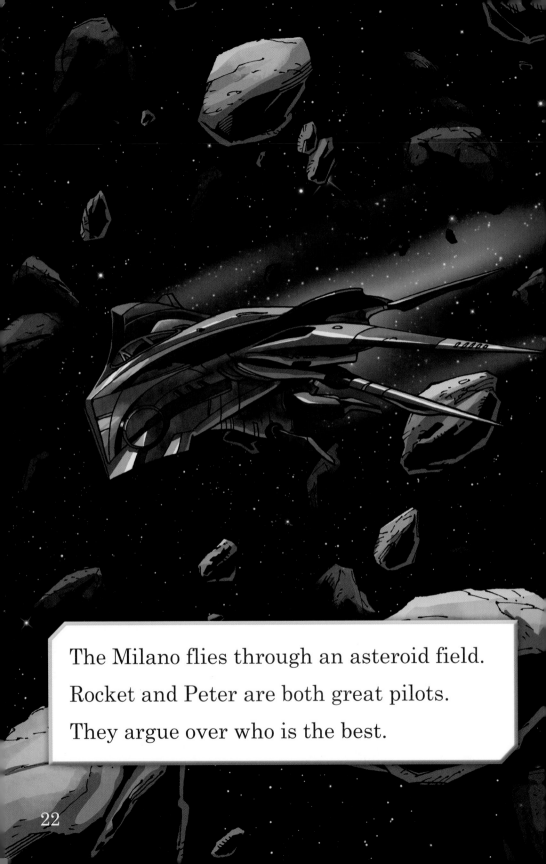

The Milano flies through an asteroid field.
Rocket and Peter are both great pilots.
They argue over who is the best.

The Guardians land on a nearby planet.

They need a plan.

How can they escape Ayesha

and her ships for good?

Soon, they meet Ego and Mantis.
Ego says that he is Peter's father.

Mantis helps Ego, and she likes
the Guardians a lot.

Yondu is the leader
of the Ravagers.
He helped raise Peter
while Ego was away.
Yondu and Peter do not
get along well anymore.

The Ravagers attack the Guardians! There is a fight, but Peter, Gamora, and Drax are away!

Yondu beats Rocket.

His arrow flies wherever he tells it.

Nebula has a plan.

She surprises everyone

and captures Yondu and Rocket!

Luckily, Groot is a great dancer.
The Ravagers think he is funny
and let him go.
They think he is harmless.

Groot helps his friends.

They need to fly to another planet.

Can Peter, Drax, Gamora, Rocket, and Groot run forever?
Will the Guardians stay out of trouble?